Grandmother and the Runaway Shadow

LIZ ROSENBERG

Illustrated by BETH PECK

Harcourt Brace & Company

San Diego   New York   London

To my grandma Dorothy, who sent me the dream,
and to Grandma Mimi, Grandpa Ben, Pappy Abe,
and all the other grandparents—and their shadows.

—L. R.

To the memory of my Grandmother Bessie Rabinowitz
and for her daughters,
Jeanette, Sylvia, Florence, and my mother, Esther

—B. P.

Library of Congress Cataloging-in-Publication-Data
Rosenberg, Liz.
Grandmother and the runaway shadow/Liz Rosenberg;
illustrated by Beth Peck.—1st ed.
p. cm.
Summary: Relates how Grandmother, accompanied by a
mischievous shadow, emigrated from Russia to the United States.
ISBN 0-15-200948-5
[1. Emigration and immigration—Fiction. 2. Shadows—Fiction.
3. Grandmothers—Fiction. I. Peck, Beth, ill. II. Title.
PZ7.R71894Gr 1996
[E]—dc20 95-7603

First edition
A B C D E

The illustrations in this book were done in oils on canvas.
The display type was set in Blackfriar.
The text type was set in Stempel Garamond.
Color separations were made by Bright Arts, Ltd., Singapore.
Printed and bound by Tien Wah Press, Singapore
This book was printed with soya-based inks on Leykam recycled
paper, which contains more than 20 percent postconsumer waste
and has a total recycled content of at least 50 percent.
Production supervision by Warren Wallerstein and Ginger Boyer
Designed by Lydia D'moch

A NOTE ABOUT THIS BOOK

Growing up, I heard many stories about the Old Country. All of my ancestors—grandparents and great-grandparents—were Eastern European Jews. Many left because of the pogroms—times of persecution when Jewish people found their lives and their homes in danger. Often they would flee secretly, and in the middle of the night, as Grandmother and the runaway shadow did in this story.

My mother's father, Grandpa Ben—used to tell me how he crossed by boat from Russia to America, alone with his crippled sister. It was a great adventure to him then, and he didn't know enough to be scared. They were sometimes so hungry on the journey, he used to say, that they would eat hay meant for the animals aboard ship. "But," he would add, when I started to look sad, "it tasted great! Just like chop suey!" My husband's grandmother told me the story of kissing the ground when she first reached America, she was so grateful to be there.

Beth Peck's maternal grandmother, Bess Rabinowitz, for whom she was named, was born in a small town on the Polish-Russian border. She came to America in 1909, at the age of twelve, with her younger sister to meet their father, who was already here. She came in steerage, withstood illness on her journey, and once here found work in a hairpiece factory and later in a garment factory. She came with a spirit and optimism she is remembered for even today.

At the end of the nineteenth century and the beginning of the twentieth, waves of such immigrants arrived in the United States. Many of them came through Ellis Island, also known as the "Isle of Tears." They came from all around the world. Most of them had to learn new customs and a new language—English. Many had to learn a new name for themselves, something that sounded more "American." But the truth is that all Americans are immigrants, except the Native Americans. As newcomers, we all depend on help and kindness.

The woman above in the feathered hat is my Grandma Mimi—short for Miriam. She's my father's mother. Her people came from Hungary and Poland and Russia. She was a schoolteacher at a time when few women had educations, much less gave them! She was a tiny woman with a very strong spirit. Her first day of teaching, the guard at the high school gate said, "Little girl, you're much too small to be going to high school." But she stood her ground till he let her in to teach!

Below is a photograph of the artist's grandmother, which she kept before her as she painted the art for this book. Illustrating this book rekindled Beth's interest in hearing family stories of her Jewish heritage. While I wrote this story without knowing Beth, her family's stories are similar to this story, including leaving Russia by crossing a field in the middle of the night.

The story of *Grandmother and the Runaway Shadow* could have come from any one of the stories we heard growing up. I believe it came from all of them. It's good to remember the past, to feel yourself rooted in a part of it. Sometimes I think I am my grandparents' shadow. One way or another, we all find ourselves in new situations, relying on kind strangers, our own courage, and a little good luck. Life is so full of journeys!

When my grandmother came to this country, a runaway shadow came with her.

You've never heard of a runaway shadow? Well, in those days the old country was full of such things. Times were so bad that even a poor shadow would run off, especially in the middle of the night. Those were the days when the Cossacks would ride into the village, shouting and waving torches. The villagers ran for their lives, as fast and as far as their feet could carry them.

My grandmother and the runaway shadow met one such night in the middle of a potato field in the middle of nowhere. "I'm going to America," my grandmother said.

"I will go with you," said the runaway shadow.

"I'll pack my bag," said my grandmother.

"I have nothing to pack," said the runaway shadow. "But I'll wait for you."

And from that day on, my grandmother told me afterward, she was never completely alone.

On the long boat ride over, children cried and parents scolded.
My grandmother leaned at the rail and watched the choppy waves,
where the runaway shadow glided alongside the boat like a bird.

And when the boat finally landed in America, my grandmother was so grateful she fell to her knees and kissed the ground, while the runaway shadow lay on its back, pretending not to care, and gazed up at the new, tall buildings.

That day, my grandmother looked for a place to live. The runaway
shadow tagged behind. As soon as it heard the landlady's loud voice on
the stairway, it shrank back.

So my grandmother sat down and explained that the landlady was a very nice woman. She could tell by her eyes.

And my grandmother turned out to be right.

That's because my grandmother looked on the bright side of things. The runaway shadow tended to look on the dark side. My grandmother was serious. She worked hard. The shadow was—unpredictable—one moment mischievous, gloomy the next.

Were they different? As different as day and night. But that's how it is sometimes even with the best of friends.

My grandmother loved the bustle of the city. She gazed happily into shop windows, while the runaway shadow shifted from one foot to the other beside her. When she stopped too long, the runaway shadow pulled on her coat sleeve. When the shadow dawdled behind, climbing fences and lampposts, she waited for it to catch up. She walked like a queen, down the middle of the sidewalk, while the shadow raced along with one foot in the gutter, and one in the street, scaring the horses.

At the Littman Street Garment Factory, my grandmother sewed buttons on coats and flounces on dresses or trimmings on hats late into the night.

In summer it was hot; in winter it was drafty. Mr. Littman, the owner, was always in a back room, yelling. Mr. Gould, the foreman, never smiled. No one talked, no one joked, till the runaway shadow stretched out on the floor underneath my grandmother's table and told funny stories that made all the women laugh.

One day the foreman appeared at the table. "Who did this?" he thundered. He held up a blue felt hat trimmed with a green velvet ribbon. At first my grandmother was too frightened to speak. But the runaway shadow gave her a little nudge from behind.

"I did," she admitted.

The foreman glared at her. But the runaway shadow stood at her back, straight and unwavering. "I thought they looked good together," my grandmother said.

"They do look good," said the foreman. So my grandmother got a ten-dollar bonus, and the hat got a new model number— style number 43.

Once a month, my grandmother and the runaway shadow went to the Garment Workers' dances. My grandmother wore her best dress and her hair gleamed like copper. She had her choice of eager partners, but she chose one tall young man with laughing eyes and a careless slouch, who later became my grandfather—though the runaway shadow outdanced them all. No one else could bend so low or leap so high and wild.

They came home from those dances tired and happy. Then just before bed, my grandmother would have her tea and a banana sandwich. The shadow wouldn't eat at all; just wait patiently for her to finish.

Then up, up the long skinny stairs they would climb. My grandmother went first, holding a candle. The runaway shadow trailed behind like the train of a gown.

In their tiny bedroom under the eaves, the runaway shadow told scary stories or made animal shapes on the walls. Sometimes my grandmother would sing the old songs—quietly, of course, so as not to wake the landlady.

They were best friends, despite their differences. And after they
had talked over the day's events, their memories of the old country,
and their hopes and plans for the future, they would hold hands in
the darkness and go to sleep.